Disney Before the Story

Mulan's SECRET PLAN

By
TESSA ROEHL

Illustrated By
DENISE SHIMABUKURO

Disney PRESS
Los Angeles • New York

For Myna
—T.R.

Chapter 1
A Little Excitement

On the first day of school, Mulan woke up before the sun. This was not unusual, as Mulan always rose before dawn—she had to in order to complete her chores before breakfast. But this morning felt different. Today she was full of energy, as if everything in front of her were a challenge she couldn't wait to conquer. She wasn't just finishing chores before the sun rose—she was *racing* the sun, determined to move faster than the light could streak through the sky.

Mulan fed Little Brother, who barked in appreciation. "I'll have all sorts of stories to tell you later," she told her dog. In the chicken coop, Mulan scattered feed on the ground, dreaming about what the day might have in store: Would she learn math today? Writing? She gathered up eggs from the coop: *One*,

two, *three*, she counted as the hens waddled toward their breakfast. She balanced the eggs carefully in her arms as she ran back toward her house, across the moon bridge, and over the pond.

Mulan skipped over the last few garden stones and leaped up the steps of her house into the kitchen, almost tripping over Little Brother. One of the eggs flew out from where she was clutching it against her robe, but she swooped down and caught it with her left hand before it cracked on the ground.

Mulan looked up to see her mother pouring tea for Grandmother Fa, who was seated at the table. Both women were laughing as they watched Mulan.

"Are you trying to ruin an old lady's breakfast, Mulan?" Grandmother Fa asked. Mulan's mother set down the teapot and took the eggs, cradling them more gently than Mulan had.

"Never, Grandmother. I haven't broken an egg yet, have I?" Mulan joined her at the table.

"I do sometimes wonder how that's possible," her mother said, shaking her head as she prepared breakfast.

"I'm challenging myself." Mulan grinned. "Father is always saying we should challenge ourselves. That's how we learn."

"If your father were here," her mother said, "I think he would add that challenging yourself can mean more than jumping across ponds and leaping high fences."

"And playing catch with our breakfast!" Grandmother Fa smiled over her tea.

"But Father is away fighting in the war, and we haven't heard from him in more than a month," Mulan said, a little sadly.

"Your father may not be sitting at this table, but his honor is still here. All of his lessons, in one way or another, lead back to honoring yourself, and honoring your family," her grandmother said.

Mulan always wanted to honor her brave father. She perked up. "Maybe going to school today will help me understand Father's lessons better. And I'll learn even more to show him when he returns!"

Grandmother Fa and Mulan's mother exchanged a look. The room was quiet for a few moments as they all sat down to eat.

"Mulan," her mother said finally. Mulan looked up from her breakfast. "Remember that this may not be the kind of school you are expecting. You will learn things—important things. But they won't be the same things your father learned. It won't be quite like the school the boys attend. And the lessons are only for six weeks."

Mulan knew this. Her mother and grandmother had been cautioning her about it ever since they announced that Mulan would start attending a class with the other village girls.

"I know, Mother," Mulan said. "But I can still be excited, can't I?"

"Yes," her mother replied. She squeezed her daughter's hand. "You certainly can."

Her grandmother winked. "A little excitement never hurts."

* * *

After breakfast, Mulan's mother and grand-mother escorted Mulan from their home to the village. Mulan's village was small enough that she knew most of the people, but she didn't know everyone. She was often busy at home doing chores and spending time with her family, so she did not go into the village every day.

When she did have a chance to venture out, she loved seeing the sights of the world beyond her home's walls. Stalls sold fresh fish brought in on carts from the neighboring town. Ladies walked around with baskets, buying food for their families. Usually, most exciting of all was catching a glimpse of the village schoolhouse and the small parade of students entering for lessons. Today, for once, Mulan was focused on what *she* would be learning when she walked into school, rather than on what the boys would be learning.

But to her surprise, her mother and grandmother led her past the school and through the village to a house, where they stopped outside the gate. Mulan knew this house. Mei, a girl just one year older than Mulan, lived there. It was one of the largest homes in the village, though Mulan had never been inside.

Mulan gave her mother a confused look.

"I told you, Mulan. It's a different kind of school," her mother said.

"But . . ." Mulan glanced back toward the schoolhouse, seeing the last of the boys trickle through the door.

Grandmother Fa placed a hand on her back as though she could sense Mulan's concern. "You will be learning here."

Mulan took a breath and nodded. What did it matter where she learned? She would be a student. Here.

And then another sight made her heart lift. Her friend Na was walking up the path, alongside her mother. Mulan waved. She felt better already, knowing she would have

a friend. As Na's mother greeted Mulan's mother and grandmother, suddenly Mulan couldn't wait to go inside.

"Ready?" Mulan asked Na.

"If you are!" Na said.

The group opened the gate and walked through the courtyard of Mei's house. It was larger than the courtyard at Mulan's home, though it, too, had a temple, a pond, a moon bridge, and rising beyond it all, the family home.

The girls were led inside the main house and into a large room. Seated on woven mats on the floor were Mei and another girl her age named Chen. Mulan also saw two other girls whom she didn't know well, Ying and Jin. There was no teacher there yet.

Mulan turned back to the door. Her mother and grandmother smiled, their faces encouraging. Mulan felt the first small flutter of nerves in her throat, but she wanted to be brave. She waved goodbye, and they left with Na's mother. The six girls were alone.

Mulan, now seated next to Na, examined the room properly for the first time. The girls faced a table with a collection of objects on top. There were a few teapots. A bag of rice next to a small bowl of cooked rice. Several pieces of paper, which Mulan was itching to touch. She'd never had the chance to learn to

write. She closed her eyes, imagining what it might feel like to be the one who let ink flow onto paper. When she opened them, she spotted something else on the table that made her heart thump harder.

"Na, look—an abacus!" When her father was home, Mulan loved watching him slide beads around the contraption as he used it to solve math problems.

"Oh," Na breathed. "We'll get to learn math!"

"I can't wait," Mulan said, grinning. "And did you see the paper? I'll bet we learn writing, too!"

"What kind of lessons do you suppose could come from the teapots?" Na asked.

Mulan was about to suggest that perhaps the teapots and the rice were set out for lunch when a soft breeze ruffled the hair on her neck. A woman entered the room. Her face was powdered white. Her lips were pursed tightly together and colored with bright red paint. Her hair was piled high on top of her head. Her arms crossed inside the sleeves of her robe so her hands were hidden. The buzz of excitement in the air vanished as the woman took her place behind the table in front of the girls. Her figure was slight, but considering the look of steel on her face, Mulan had a feeling this woman would be a match for any of the village's toughest warriors. When she opened her mouth to speak, the words that came out were not what Mulan had expected.

"Greetings, girls. I am your matchmaker."

Chapter 2
The Matchmaker

The buzz in the room was back. The girls whispered to each other.

"A matchmaker?" Mulan asked Na under her breath.

"Already?" Na was interrupted by a sharp rap on the front table.

"Silence!" the matchmaker demanded.

The six girls halted their conversations and sat up straight.

"I see that manners are something we will need to work on," the matchmaker said, frowning. She moved her eyes from Mulan, to Na, to the rest of the girls, one by one. The quiet in the room made Mulan uncomfortable. As if she might be making a mistake by breathing.

Finally, the matchmaker continued. "Do you all know what a matchmaker does?"

The girls looked at each other, nervous.

"Well?" the woman asked.

Mulan spoke, anxious to break the silence. "A matchmaker comes to the village and—"

The matchmaker put a finger to her lips.

Mulan stopped talking. "What is your name, child?"

"Mulan."

"Mulan, you will raise your hand when you'd like to speak and wait until I call on you. It is impolite for a girl to speak unless she is asked to do so."

Mulan slumped down, her face warm.

"Yes?" The matchmaker gestured toward the back of the room. Ying had her arm raised.

"A matchmaker's duty is to evaluate a potential bride, judge her family and skills, and find her a suitable husband," Ying said clearly and confidently.

"One could say a matchmaker's duty is to find a suitable wife for a groom," the matchmaker said. "But that will do."

Ying lowered her arm, a small smirk on her face. Mulan felt even worse now for missing her first chance to impress the matchmaker. Ying's answer was the one Mulan had been planning to give before the matchmaker silenced her.

"And that is why I'm here. In recent years, I've found that in many villages, potential brides are nowhere near where they ought to be in terms of household skills, culture, and education." The matchmaker paused, fanning her face. "A matchmaker is only as good as the matches she makes."

She snapped her fan shut and pointed it at the girls. "So we are starting when you are young. Even though you are not yet of matchmaking age, and won't be for several years, now is the time you are most impressionable. Now is the time to begin your training. I don't know what kind of education you are getting at home, but here, you will learn everything you need to know."

The room stayed quiet. But Mulan could

sense a bit of the excitement returning. They were going to learn after all! Mulan was suspicious, though, of the last bit the matchmaker had said: it sounded like she was doubting the education the girls were getting at home from their families. Mulan had learned a great deal from her parents and grandmother. She could take care of the farm, she could prepare tea and some meals, and she even—when her parents weren't watching—liked to imitate her father's punching technique, using a bag of leaves for practice.

"By the end of our six weeks together," the matchmaker said, "you will be more elegant, more polite, and more knowledgeable.

And when you're old enough to marry, the *most* elegant, the *most* polite, and the *most* knowledgeable among you . . . that's who will get the best match of all."

Mulan raised her hand.

"Yes?" The matchmaker pointed at her.

Mulan gulped. All heads turned in her direction. "Matchmaker, what makes a match the best?"

The matchmaker snorted. "Why, the best match is a husband with the greatest wealth and the highest status, of course." She picked up a bowl of rice from the table and then noticed Mulan's hand was raised again. "You have another question?"

Mulan continued. "But what if . . . even though the groom has the most money . . . what if *I* don't think he's the best match? What if he's not nice? Or what if he isn't brave?"

The matchmaker set the bowl down and narrowed her eyes at Mulan.

"It is not about *nice*, child. It is about what will bring you, your village, and your family the most honor. Does that matter to you?"

Mulan nodded.

"Honor is more important than . . . *nice*, are we agreed?" the matchmaker asked.

Mulan nodded even harder. She couldn't

imagine not bringing honor to her family.

"Then you will have a chance to prove this. At the end of our lessons, we will have a competition in which you will demonstrate the skills you've learned," the matchmaker said. "And the one whom I deem most accomplished will gain extra favor, which will give her a leg up when it is time to make her match in a few years."

Mulan bit her lip. She had a feeling she would need all the extra favor she could get with this matchmaker.

"You will need to pay very close attention. For some of you, these skills will come naturally, and for others . . . well,

unfortunately, they won't," the matchmaker said as she picked up the bowl again.

Mulan scowled. So what if she didn't know something naturally? She knew how to work hard. And she bet the other girls in the class did, too.

"Our first lesson," the matchmaker said, holding up the bowl, "is something you will be doing day after day. Cooking the perfect bowl of rice."

Panic struck Mulan's heart. To her right, Na looked just as fearful. *Perfect?* Mulan had watched her grandmother and mother make rice every day for most of her life, but she'd never tried it all by herself! "Do you know how to make perfect rice?" Mulan asked Na, leaning close to her.

Na shook her head. "No! Do you?"

"In *silence.*" The matchmaker glared at Mulan and Na.

Mulan and Na pulled away from each other reluctantly and stood in line with the rest of the girls to get their supplies: bowls, a small portion of rice, and a kettle of water.

One of Mei's family attendants came in to start the fire, and the girls took turns boiling their water and beginning their rice. Mulan wished she could chat with Na about the steps she was taking. And she was bothered by the fact that this didn't seem to be much of a lesson at all, but rather a test. Wouldn't she be more likely to make perfect rice if the matchmaker had provided them with instructions?

Finally, Mulan took the lid off her rice. She tasted it, hoping that was allowed. It wasn't the *worst* rice she'd ever had. It certainly wasn't perfect, though. It had an equal balance of mushy, overcooked rice grains along with hard, slightly crunchy ones. But there were plenty of grains that felt just right on her tongue. She decided it was a success, all things considered.

"We will now taste the rice together," the matchmaker announced. Luckily, she hadn't noticed that Mulan had already snuck a bite. The matchmaker tasted rice from each bowl, and then let the girls taste them all, too. Na's rice was slightly better than Mulan's—mostly cooked well, but it definitely still had a few crunchy bits. Chen's and Jin's rice was about the same. Mei's rice, however, was so overcooked it was hard to see the individual grains at all.

Ying's bowl was the last to be tasted. Once Mulan had a bite, it was clear that *this* was perfect rice. Until she'd tasted Ying's rice, Mulan hadn't even realized that her own mother and grandmother weren't making perfect rice!

The matchmaker knew this bowl was perfect, too. "Very good," she said. Mulan thought she saw a hint of a smile on the woman's face. Ying gave another smirk of satisfaction.

Mulan sat back down on her mat and peeked over at Ying. She would be the one to beat in the matchmaker's lessons if Mulan wanted to make the best match and, in turn, bring the most honor to her family.

Chapter 3
Tea and Sympathy

Mulan entered the courtyard of her home, passing through the moon gate and into the kitchen where her mother and grandmother were waiting, sipping tea. Little Brother greeted her by sticking his cold nose in her hand.

"Granddaughter!" Grandmother Fa put down her tea and patted the mat next to her. "Come, tell us all about it."

Mulan sat down and gratefully accepted the tea her mother poured. "School was . . . interesting."

"Interesting?" Her grandmother clucked her tongue. "After the way you jumped around this morning, you'll have to tell us more than that."

Mulan gulped her tea and felt the hot liquid coat her throat. She imagined it was fire, filling her up and making her strong. "We made rice."

"That's not something you've done on your own yet," her mother said. "Aren't you pleased that you're already learning something new?"

"Well, the matchmaker didn't exactly *teach* us how to make rice," Mulan said. "She watched us and judged us on making rice."

Grandmother Fa chuckled. "Sounds like your matchmaker isn't much easier on you than mine was."

Mulan looked up in surprise. "You had a matchmaker, Grandmother?"

"Why, of course I did. So did your mother," her grandmother said. Mulan's mother nodded.

"Did you have to go to a class like this?" Mulan asked.

Grandmother Fa shook her head. "This is not a common practice. But it might have been better if it were! Why, I was terrified the day I met my matchmaker. I was only a few years older than you. Perhaps if I had taken a class at your age, I would have been more prepared."

"*You* were terrified?" Mulan asked. She was fascinated by this idea of her grandmother, young enough to visit a matchmaker. But even more so, she was fascinated by the idea of her grandmother being terrified of anything.

"Oh, yes," her grandmother continued. "The matchmaker was studying my skills around the house, the way I was dressed, my family . . . everything. And her evaluation was going to determine who I would marry—determine the rest of my life!"

Mulan frowned. "It doesn't seem very fair that someone who doesn't know you would get to decide that."

Mulan's mother poured more tea. "It didn't turn out so bad, did it, though?" she asked Grandmother Fa.

"Not at all," Mulan's grandmother said. "If I hadn't been matched with your grandfather, we wouldn't have your father, Mulan. And then we wouldn't have you. The matchmaker is an expert for a reason."

"Were you scared of the matchmaker, too, Mother?" Mulan asked.

Her mother's cheeks turned pink. "Nothing had ever scared me more," she admitted. "But Mulan, you are brave. Much braver than I was. There's nothing to worry about. This class will help you improve the basic skills you already have. Listen to what the matchmaker teaches you and follow your instincts. They will always lead you down the right path."

Grandmother Fa reached out to touch Mulan's mother on the shoulder. "Very wise. Your mother is right, Mulan."

Mulan relaxed. Sitting with her family, safe in her comfortable house with their afternoon tea, had a way of making her feel as though troubles couldn't get through the courtyard walls. And hearing her mother and grandmother admit that they'd had fears in the past, too, made her feel less alone. If they could do it, she could do it.

She gave Little Brother an absentminded pat, thinking about the matchmaker's lessons. *I'll learn everything I can, as much as I can, and work hard to make sure I'm the best in the class,* she thought.

Her mother's voice pulled her back to

the present. "We received good news today," Mulan heard her say. "Your father should be coming home soon."

Mulan gripped her teacup with both hands, nearly shattering it in her excitement. "Really? Is the war over?"

"Not quite yet, but they no longer need so many fighters," Grandmother Fa said. "Your father is beginning his journey back home."

What a fantastic surprise! It had been almost a year since Mulan had seen her father. She missed him terribly, though she knew he'd been bringing their family honor by fighting in the war. She couldn't think of a better welcome-home gift for her father than doing well in the matchmaker's lessons and bringing him some honor in return.

Chapter 4
A Rice Makeover

The next day, Na met Mulan outside Mulan's gate, and the girls walked to Mei's house together. They took turns guessing what task they would face that day. Their answers quickly grew silly, going from preparing dumplings to standing on their heads to trapping giant pandas. By the time they reached Mei's house, they were giggling so hard they could barely breathe. But once they entered the classroom, their giggles stopped. It was clear that this room was not a place for giggling, or for having fun of any kind.

Mulan and Na sat on the same mats as the day before. To their disappointment, they saw that in front of each seat was another portion of uncooked rice. Mulan wondered if today they would learn from the matchmaker how to prepare the perfect rice that Ying had made.

Before she could wonder much more, the matchmaker entered the room and the girls gave her their complete attention.

"Making and applying cosmetics are

valuable skills for a lady," the matchmaker began. She gestured toward her face. "As you can see, when done properly, makeup can bring out a woman's beauty—highlight her best features, and hide her worst."

Mulan wasn't sure she agreed. From where she sat, the harsh white powder made the matchmaker look stiff and mean.

The matchmaker continued lecturing the girls about the cosmetic styles gaining popularity in other villages: waxy red lip coloring, thick black lines around the eyes, plucked and painted eyebrows, decorations on the foreheads and cheeks. Mulan didn't know why anyone bothered with such things!

After an hour of speaking about all the different ways a lady could apply makeup, the matchmaker finally arrived at the day's activity. "The powder I have on my face is made from rice. So today we will be grinding the rice into a powder you can wear. Please choose a partner to whom you will apply the powder—but you will each be making your own. Begin!"

Mulan and Na partnered up. Again, Mulan found it odd that the matchmaker was asking them to perform a task without first teaching them how to do it. Mulan had never made or worn makeup, and she knew Na hadn't, either. Had any of the girls done this? Was this what other mothers and grandmothers were teaching their daughters at home while Mulan was gathering eggs and feeding the animals?

Nevertheless, Mulan was going to try her best. If turning rice into makeup would bring honor to her family, she'd do it, even if it seemed a little silly to her.

Mulan took a wooden rolling pin and a solid hardwood board and placed her rice grains on the surface, as she saw the other girls doing. Crushing the rice into a fine powder was not easy. The grains kept

slipping out from under her rolling pin. No matter how hard she pressed, jammed, and shoved the rice against the board, it refused to transform into a silky powder. She peered at Na's work space and saw that her friend was having similar problems. Mulan kept attacking the rice, aware all the time that the matchmaker was pacing around the room watching them.

"Girls, you've been working with the rice long enough. Begin applying the makeup now," the matchmaker called to her students.

Mulan and Na stopped grinding. By now Mulan's rice was slightly powdery, but still quite chunky.

"You first?" Na asked Mulan.

Mulan sighed. "Okay," she said. She scooped her fingers into her rice mixture and swiped some of the rough powder over Na's cheek. A trace of white clung to her skin, but the heavier rice pieces fell to the floor. Na and Mulan looked at the fallen rice and both stifled giggles.

Mulan knew that she did not have enough of the fine powder to cover more than one of Na's cheekbones. She needed a way to make the bigger pieces stick so that at least Na's face would be covered. It didn't seem like the matchmaker would be giving them any tips, as she'd stopped to admire her own makeup in a small bronze mirror.

Thinking quickly, Mulan dipped her fingers in a pail of water nearby and then scooped up more of the rice mixture. When she wiped it on this time, the water helped the heavier pieces cling to Na's face. Unfortunately, it was more like a paste than a powder. When Mulan finished, Na's face was covered in a splotchy, goopy white mess.

When it was Na's turn, she mimicked what Mulan had done with the water. The wet, sloppy makeup felt strange on Mulan's face. When Na was finished, she tilted her head, studying Mulan.

"Is that what I look like?" she asked,

taking in Mulan's appearance. The two girls leaned over the water pail to see their reflections. As they moved, clumps of rice plopped and splashed into the water. Mulan and Na erupted into the giggles they'd been holding in for the entire lesson. Mulan laughed so hard that she knocked against the pail, spilling some water on the ground.

"Ahem!"

Mulan and Na sprang up. The match-maker stood at the front of the room, hands on hips. Mei and Chen looked worse than Mulan and Na; there was no powder on their faces at all, only whole grains of rice that dropped off their skin, one by one, breaking the silence with a steady *plink, plink, plink* as they hit the ground.

Ying and Jin were a different sight. Jin, who was wearing Ying's makeup, had a face dusted in fine, white powder. It looked nearly identical to the matchmaker's, without the eyebrow and lip coloring. Ying's face was almost as perfect; Jin had mostly managed to grind the rice into a powder, with just a few small flecks of grains remaining.

Mulan could see the admiration in the matchmaker's eyes as she inspected Ying's and Jin's faces. After a few moments, she turned back toward Mulan, Na, Mei, and Chen. "While you were giggling and playing with your rice, these two were completing their lesson successfully. These classes are not a time for silliness and acting like children," the matchmaker said.

How else could we act? Mulan thought to herself. She knew she had been trying hard . . . she couldn't help it if it turned out so funny.

"If you don't improve," the matchmaker said, pointing at the rest of the girls, "Ying may be the only one who's suitable to match with a husband when she's of age."

Mulan felt the mood in the room sink. It wasn't the idea of not having a husband—Mulan still wasn't sure how much she cared about *that*. But another lesson had passed, and she hadn't come any closer to impressing the matchmaker and securing future honor for her family. And she probably never would, as long as her skills lagged so far behind Ying's.

Quietly, the girls washed up and left Mei's house. As Mulan headed home, her gaze drifted toward the schoolhouse. The boys were outside, practicing martial arts with their instructor. Mulan admired the way their arms moved with grace. The way their legs kicked with purpose.

Mulan knew the boys weren't learning martial arts so they would be able to please *their* eventual matches. She yearned to join the boys as she watched them practice a leap-kick combination, over and over. Who wanted to spend a day cooped up inside, next to each other but alone, crushing rice into powder for makeup, when it was possible to be leaping, kicking, and working as a team?

Chapter 5
Ying's Secret

The lessons of the next few days unfolded much like the first two had. Mulan was determined to try her hardest and not lose hope. But it was becoming clear that the matchmaker was not much of a teacher. Every day the girls faced a new challenge, and every day one girl did a bit better than the others.

Na, who often helped her mother mend

her younger sister's clothes, had the strongest embroidery skills, but was banned from showing anyone her stitching method. Mei was a talented painter, but the matchmaker scolded her when she tried to show the girls how to blend colors. Jin was especially good at mixing herbs for tea, but the matchmaker forbade her to share her recipe. Chen knew how to form many of the brushstrokes for calligraphy, but didn't dare share her knowledge behind the matchmaker's back.

Despite how well the girls did at each task, however, Ying was *always* the best. There was no doubt who would win the competition at the end of the class. Na's stitches were excellent, but Ying embroidered more flowers than the other girls combined. Mei's painting was lovely, but Ying's looked like it could be sold at a market. Jin's tea was fragrant and rich, but Ying's tasted like it could be served in a fine teahouse. Chen's calligraphy characters were neat, but Ying's were perfect. Mulan thought she and the other girls might have a chance to be as good as Ying was if only they could truly practice these skills. If they could help each other as a team.

An idea was beginning to form in Mulan's head. She wasn't sure if the others would go for it—especially Ying—but Mulan knew something had to change. As her mother had warned her, this was not like the boys' school—the girls were supposed to be competing against each other. Still, Mulan hoped the others also wanted to really learn something.

On the day Mulan decided to tell the others about her idea, the girls arrived before the matchmaker. There were baskets of fuzzy white balls and trays of wriggling white-and-brown-striped worms on the matchmaker's table. Mulan recognized them as silkworms. Na, Mei, and Chen wrinkled their noses at the sight of the worms, and Jin jumped.

"What's the matter?" Mulan asked.

"As many times as I've helped my mother feed silkworms, I'll never get used to how . . . *ugly* those creepy-crawly things are!" Jin shuddered.

"Who would think beautiful silk would come from those?" Na added.

The other girls were murmuring in agreement when Ying entered the classroom. Mulan noticed she didn't bother to peek at the front of the room to check out the assignment for the day. Mulan wondered what it must feel like to be so confident that you were good at *everything*.

"What if we aren't making silk?" Chen asked, a twinkle in her eye.

"What do you mean?" Jin asked.

Chen continued, teasing Jin. "What if the matchmaker makes us turn them into a gourmet meal? What if we have to *eat them*?"

Jin shrieked. "We wouldn't—would we?!"

Mulan laughed. "No, don't worry. Not without cooking them first."

Jin's face turned whiter than the day they had practiced applying rice powder makeup.

"I'm only joking!" Mulan said. "The matchmaker would certainly make us eat them raw," she added with a grin.

"Excuse me." The matchmaker's voice cut through the room. Mulan froze. She'd been so caught up in laughing with her friends, she hadn't noticed the matchmaker enter.

The matchmaker sneered at Mulan. "Silk weaving is one of the most treasured and special skills in China. Silk thread can be used for clothes, for paper, for fishing line, to trade for other items . . . If you are skilled in raising silkworms and crafting silk, it could benefit you and your family in countless ways. It is not a *joke*."

Mulan blushed. As if she needed to disappoint the matchmaker further!

The matchmaker continued to speak about the marvel and beauty of silk, explaining how it came from silkworms that fed on mulberry leaves, and how merchants would travel for miles and miles to purchase the fabric. At least some of this was information Mulan didn't know, and she paid attention with interest, despite her embarrassment. The lectures the matchmaker gave were usually the only time Mulan ended up learning anything.

When it was time for the activity of the day, the matchmaker had each girl take a small reel and a bucket of the fuzzy silkworm cocoons. After soaking the cocoons in hot water, the girls unraveled the filaments onto their reels. Mulan worked, her nimble fingers twisting the fibers into threads. She had always loved watching her grandmother weave silk, enchanted by the fact that from these worms and their cocoons, something so unexpected could be produced.

When the matchmaker finally called, "Time is up, girls," Mulan had wound a tight figure eight of silk. Na had not managed nearly so much.

A thrill ran through Mulan as she admired her work. She was certain that she had made more thread than the rest of the girls . . . until she saw where the matchmaker was now standing: next to Ying, who had managed to reel more than double what Mulan had produced. How was that even possible? Mulan had unwound all the cocoons she'd been given!

But the matchmaker was praising Ying again, without even a glance in Mulan's direction. Mulan supposed she should be proud of what she had accomplished, but now another day's lessons were over and still no one was close to equaling Ying. Even if there was no besting her, it would be nice to at least *learn* some of what she knew. Mulan could see a similar disappointment in Jin's, Chen's, Na's, and Mei's faces as they headed toward the door. Mulan remembered that she wanted to speak to them about her idea. "Wait up," Mulan called to the girls.

She gathered her belongings, pushing down her disappointment with the day's lesson. When she turned around to leave, she ran smack into Ying, who was looking into her bag on her way out. Both girls stumbled, falling to the ground.

"I'm sorry!" Mulan said, reaching out to help Ying pick up what she'd dropped. "But I'm glad you're still here, Ying. I wanted to talk to you and the other girls . . ." Mulan's voice trailed off as she noticed what she was holding. It was a hank of silk thread. And it had not come from the class's silkworms. It had come from Ying's bag.

Ying had cheated.

Chapter 6
The Idea

"**G**ive me that," Ying said in a shrill whisper.

Mulan handed the spool back to Ying. "Is that how you did so well today?" Mulan whispered back. "Did you even make any of your own thread?"

"Please don't tell the matchmaker," Ying said softly, placing the spool in the bag.

Mulan could see her eyes were full of fear. "Please."

"Have you been doing this all along?" Mulan asked. "While the rest of us have been working so hard? We've all been trying our best!"

Ying didn't answer. She looked so frightened. Mulan felt sorry for her, even though she was also very angry.

"I won't tell her," Mulan sighed. "But it's not fair."

"I know." Ying's voice broke and she bowed her head. Mulan saw a tear hit the floor as Ying closed her bag, stood up, and fled the small classroom.

Mulan exited, too, considering whether she should go after Ying. But Mei, Chen, Na, and Jin were lingering outside the room, waiting for Mulan.

"What was that all about?" Mei asked. "Why did Miss Perfect run off?"

Mulan chewed her lip. The other girls watched her expectantly, waiting to hear what had happened. "Well," Mulan began, "it turns out she's not so perfect. . . ." She described the encounter in the classroom with Ying and how it seemed she had somehow been cheating at her tasks by bringing finished products from home.

"I can't believe it!" Chen said when Mulan finished her story.

"I can," Na said. "No one is that good at everything!"

"You know," Jin said, "I thought something was strange when we made our rice powder. She kept turning her back to me when she was grinding the rice. I thought she was hiding her special technique from me . . . but now it all makes sense."

Mulan nodded. "She must have been spying on the matchmaker to find out what the activities were in advance." She couldn't think of how else Ying would know what to bring from home. Though it didn't explain the perfect rice on the first day.

Mei clenched her fists. "The class is in *my* house. I probably could have cheated that way if I wanted to. But I didn't. It's not fair."

"We ought to tell the matchmaker," Chen said.

"Right," Na said. "The matchmaker shouldn't let a cheater have the best match."

Her friends' words were making Mulan uncomfortable. It was true that Ying had been dishonest, but they hadn't seen the look in her eyes—it was more than fear of being caught. It was shame. And Mulan hated the

thought of bringing even more of that shame onto Ying by telling the matchmaker, especially when she had promised she wouldn't. She decided to change the subject.

"I had an idea." The other girls turned to face her. "This class . . . it feels a little weird, doesn't it?"

"What do you mean?" Na asked.

"Well," Mulan continued, "the matchmaker doesn't seem to care if we actually *learn* anything."

The other girls nodded. This gave Mulan courage to go on. "Why shouldn't we be able to learn from each other, though?"

"The matchmaker says whoever has the

best skills will get the best match," Jin said. "She's just trying to judge who's really best."

"Which is hard when someone is cheating," Mei muttered.

"But our matches won't happen for *ages*," Mulan said, trying to keep the focus on her idea rather than Ying's cheating.

"The matchmaker won't let us help each other. She's made that pretty clear," Chen said.

"Maybe she doesn't need to know," Mulan said.

"Wait. What are you saying, Mulan?" Na asked.

"I'm saying we should do something

about it," Mulan said. "Outside of class, we could teach each other what we know."

"The matchmaker will *not* like that," Mei said.

"But if we improve, how could she be angry?" Mulan asked. "We're supposed to be polite, and working together seems very polite to me. We're asked to be clever, and since we're not learning these things in class, I think it's clever to teach each other. We'll prove that we're good matches by learning all we can! Even if it's not quite in the way the matchmaker expects."

Mulan held her breath as the other girls stared at her in silence. *What if suggesting this plan was a mistake?* she thought. *What if they accuse me of trying to cheat and are angry with me just like they are with Ying?*

"I do really want to know how to make that tea, Jin," Na said. The tension broke, and the girls laughed. Mulan had convinced them.

Chapter 7
A New Lesson

The next morning, Mulan felt as excited as she had on the first day of the matchmaker's classes. She and the other girls had agreed to ask their parents for an extra hour away from home each day to spend studying. And they *would* be studying! It just wouldn't be with the matchmaker. And they would get to spend time with new friends, on top of it.

Mulan felt so energized that, while she

waited for the hens to eat their breakfast, she practiced the leap-kick combination she'd seen the village boys learning days earlier. She practiced it again on the moon bridge. And again on her way into the kitchen while holding the morning eggs—catching each one as it fell from her hands and nearly hit

the floor, then bowing at her mother's and grandmother's laughter and applause.

Over breakfast, Mulan's mother and Grandmother Fa gave her permission to spend the extra hour studying. And on her walk to Mei's house, the sight of the boys filing into school didn't make Mulan feel as envious as it had before. After all, now she felt like she was becoming a part of what they belonged to—a team.

Mulan entered the classroom and greeted Jin, Na, Chen, and Mei. Mulan noted that Ying's usual place was empty.

"My parents approved the extra study time," Na told Mulan as she sat down.

"Ours did, too!" Jin, Mei, and Chen exclaimed.

"We can start this afternoon," Mulan said. The girls buzzed and began talking over each other about their plans until Ying appeared in the doorway.

The girls quieted and turned to look at her. Ying's face reddened immediately. She hung her head, avoiding the stares, and walked to her mat next to Jin.

"We know what you did," Chen said to Ying.

Ying didn't move. Mulan whipped her head around to look at Chen.

"It's not fair to cheat," Chen said. "If you do it again, we're going to tell the matchmaker."

"Yeah," Mei, Jin, and Na chimed in. Ying still hadn't looked up. Her eyes were focused on her shoes.

Mulan felt her own face turning red. When she'd told the other girls what Ying had done, she hadn't expected that they would confront her like this. Even though Ying had cheated, Mulan didn't want her to feel embarrassed. Luckily, Chen didn't have the chance to say anything more, as the matchmaker entered the room to begin the day's class.

Throughout the matchmaker's lecture on the admonitions, an ancient scroll with lessons about manners, Ying remained as still as stone. She stumbled when it was her turn to repeat the lines from the scroll. She could barely remember three of the words, let alone a sentence or two. Mulan could tell the matchmaker was frustrated by the sudden change in her best student.

When the lesson was over, Ying hurried out of the room before Mulan could even stand up. Na whispered in Mulan's ear, "Now it's time for us to *actually* learn something." Mulan nodded and tried to get back in that brilliant mood she'd begun the day with.

The girls went to a quiet, shady glen, right outside the bustle of the village. Just as in the matchmaker's classroom, the girls had a few supplies, sat on the ground, and were eager to learn. But here, they got to have fun, too!

During their hour together, Jin taught the others about different herbs for tea using ingredients she'd brought from home. She not only taught the girls the recipe that had impressed the matchmaker, but she also showed them how to dry flowers and leaves, and demonstrated the exact right amount of time to steep each mixture in water. They didn't have a fire to boil water and taste the

tea, but that didn't stop them from learning.

As the girls said goodbye at the end of the hour, however, Mulan's mind drifted back to Ying. She felt sad that all the girls in the class were bonding and teaching each other while one was left out.

When she got home, Mulan practiced making a pot of real tea for her mother and grandmother using the recipe Jin had taught them earlier that afternoon.

"Smells delicious," Grandmother Fa said as Mulan poured the steaming liquid into small cups.

"How was your day, Mulan?" her mother asked. "You look a little troubled. Did it feel too long with the extra hour of studying?"

Mulan sighed as she reached over to scratch Little Brother's ears. She was never good at hiding her feelings from her family. Before she could help it, the whole story about Ying had come out.

"It sounds like Ying may be having the hardest time of everyone in class," Grandmother Fa said.

"But that's only because she was caught," Mulan said. "Right? Why should I feel bad when she was the one who cheated?"

"But now Ying has gone from the top of the class to being alone at the bottom. Has

anyone talked to her to ask if she's all right?"
Mulan's mother asked.

Mulan shook her head. "Not really," she
said quietly. "We talked to each other. Not
to Ying."

"Often, it's worth asking why someone
felt they had to lie in the first place. How
will you understand the answers if you don't
ask the questions?" Grandmother Fa swirled
her tea in her cup, looking into its depths as
though she could see the world inside. "And
it's always better to talk *to* someone than
about someone."

Hearing her grandmother's words, Mulan

felt ashamed for not checking on Ying the first time she'd run out of the classroom, when Mulan had discovered the silk thread. Ying might have needed someone to talk to. Mulan wished she were as wise as her mother and grandmother. There was still so much she didn't know. How could she make it better now?

Chapter 8
Another Side of Ying

The following morning, on her way to school, Mulan spotted Ying huddled near the door of a closed shop with her mother. They looked like they were having a heated discussion. Mulan crept closer, then darted around a corner where Ying and her mother would not see her.

"Your family is counting on you, Ying," Mulan could hear Ying's mother say. "If you aren't the best in the class, making sure the matchmaker remembers you in the future, what will happen to us? What will happen to me, your father, your grandfather?"

"I'm trying, Mother." Ying's voice was small. There was no trace of the confident girl Mulan had seen weeks ago when the matchmaker's lessons first began.

"How are you trying? When I saw the matchmaker yesterday, she told me you'd barely managed to memorize one word of the admonitions."

"I'm sorry," Ying said in a small voice. "I don't know how to be the best all the time."

"You will have to figure out a way,"

Ying's mother said. "Anything less will not be accepted."

Mulan's mind swirled with thoughts. She knew that the husband a matchmaker chose was important to everyone, including Mulan's own family. But Mulan's mother, father, and grandmother had never once made Mulan feel like the bride she would become was the only thing that counted.

Mulan's family valued her cleverness, her sense of humor, her love. They had never made Mulan feel that her future match mattered more than her own happiness or sense of honor. And now it was clear to Mulan that Ying's family was making her

feel the opposite. No wonder she had tried to cheat, with that kind of pressure.

Before she could second-guess herself, Mulan rounded the corner. Ying and her mother both turned, startled by the interruption.

"Good morning, Ying!" Mulan said cheerily. Ying just looked at Mulan, pale with terror.

Ying's mother stared at her daughter. "Aren't you going to introduce me to your friend?"

"M-mother," Ying stammered, "this is Mulan."

Mulan faced Ying's mother. "I'm sorry

for interrupting, but I was hoping to get your permission for something." Mulan swallowed, trying to ignore Ying's eyes growing wider by the moment. "Ying is so talented in all the skills the matchmaker teaches us. Could she possibly take an extra hour each day after our lessons to help me study?"

Ying's expression turned to one of confusion. Ying's mother frowned. "Why should she help you? It's better for Ying to excel. It's better for her to stay the best."

Mulan laughed, shaking her head. "I'm so far from ever catching up to Ying, you don't have to worry about that. Teaching me would . . ."—Mulan searched for something to say. Lying didn't exactly come naturally to her, but she wanted to help Ying—"would only help her prepare for running a household someday. With the excellent match she's sure to have, there must be a large household staff in Ying's future."

Ying's mother smiled. "This is true. But considering Ying's poor performance with the admonitions yesterday, she'll need to focus on her own improvements."

Mulan thought quickly. "You know, I was doing *so* terribly with the admonitions myself, I think I confused Ying and made her slip up. Right, Ying?" Mulan nudged

Ying, trying to send her a silent message: *Go with it!*

"That's right," Ying said slowly. "That must have been it."

"Well," Ying's mother said, "we can't have your lesser abilities dragging Ying down. If the extra hour of studying helps Ying stay on top, then you have my permission." She smoothed her daughter's hair and then walked away, leaving the girls alone.

"Why did you do that?" Ying asked Mulan once her mother was out of sight. Her eyes searched Mulan's face as though it might hold the answer. "I thought you hated me."

"I don't hate you," Mulan said. "I was angry that you cheated. But I understand what it's like to want to bring honor to your family."

"That's what I want, but it's really hard," Ying said. "My mother is always talking about how I need to make a good match. I didn't think I could deal with my family's disappointment if I wasn't the best in the class. But I was wrong to cheat. I'm sorry."

Mulan reached a hand out and placed it on Ying's shoulder. "I believe you. And I wasn't really lying about the extra studying. . . ." She explained what she and the other girls had planned.

"They probably won't want me there," Ying said. "They're pretty mad at me."

"They'll come around," Mulan said. She hoped that was true. "I do have a question, though. How did you spy on the matchmaker before the first day of class? None of us even knew who the matchmaker was before then!"

"Oh." Ying shrugged. "I didn't spy on the first day."

Mulan's mouth dropped open. "You really can make perfect rice? All by yourself?"

"I guess so!" Ying perked up.

"I think teaching us how to do that will

go a long way toward earning everyone's forgiveness."

Ying grinned. "I can do that."

And the two girls headed to the small classroom in Mei's house, together.

Chapter 9
Becoming a Team

After another day of reciting admonitions with the matchmaker, Mulan could feel the other girls watching as she left Mei's house with Ying. The moment they were outside, Mulan spoke up.

"I invited Ying to join our group," she said. Ying fidgeted nervously at her side. Mulan clasped her hand. "I want her there."

The other girls all glared at Ying. "I'm

sorry," Ying blurted. "I'm so, so sorry. I never meant to make anyone else look bad. I know it was wrong."

There was a silence that seemed to drag on forever, and Mulan began to get nervous. But then Jin stepped forward. "I forgive you," she told Ying. "You've looked really sad these past couple days. I feel like maybe you're even more upset with yourself than we are."

"I don't know," Chen said. "I'm pretty upset."

Na shifted her feet. "I didn't like what you did, Ying. But I did feel bad about excluding you."

"It felt awful," Ying admitted. "Walking in yesterday, I knew I wasn't wanted."

"I supposed we could have been nicer," Mei said. "Everyone deserves a second chance."

Chen crossed her arms. "How do we know you aren't just going to tell the matchmaker about our group so you look even better?"

Ying thought for a moment. "All I can say is that cheating made me feel incredibly lonely. And I don't ever want to feel that way again. Being the best really isn't worth it."

Chen's face softened, and she smiled.

"That's good enough for me. Let's go not be the best together."

For the next few weeks, leading up to the matchmaker's end-of-school competition, the six girls met every day. The secret meetings made Mulan feel like she and her friends had some power. They could learn despite the matchmaker's not-so-helpful "lessons," even though there was no school for the girls like there was for the boys. They weren't learning martial arts, but they were fighting in their own way.

They had to get creative with their

materials, though. Na brought scraps of fabric from home so the girls could practice tidy rows of stitches. Mulan demonstrated how an abacus worked using small pebbles on the ground. They all practiced sums until Mulan was sure any one of them would make a brilliant merchant. Ying used Jin's dried flowers and herbs to demonstrate the proper ratio for her delicious rice. The girls practiced Ying's method every night at home with their own families until they too made perfect, fluffy rice. Chen taught the others the calligraphy strokes and characters she knew by writing in the dirt with a stick. As for the admonitions, which all  the girls had trouble memorizing, Mei had a special trick to share for remembering them. It involved turning the admonitions into a very silly song, and while it certainly helped the girls with their memorization, every time they practiced, they dissolved into fits of giggles that usually didn't stop for the rest of the afternoon.

The girls also learned more about each other. Na spoke about her many younger siblings and how nice it was to spend time away, with friends her own age. Ying spoke of the pressure she felt to do well in the matchmaker's lessons. Many of the girls related to the way Ying felt. Mulan confessed how envious she had been of the boys' education and how she had wished that she had been going to a school like theirs. She even showed the girls the leap-kick combination she'd been practicing. They weren't much better at it than she was, but it was a lot of fun trying to master it together.

Truthfully, though, Mulan wasn't sorry anymore that her school had turned out differently. If it hadn't, she wouldn't be sharing

these afternoons with her new friends, studying as a team. Mulan felt proud that she
had listened to the voice inside that ques-
tioned the matchmaker. That she had found
another way to learn.

Chapter 10
The Competition

Three weeks after Mulan and the other girls began their afternoon meetings, it was time for the matchmaker's competition. All the girls had invited their families, and everyone was now gathered in Mei's courtyard, chatting politely. There was tension in the air. Mulan could only imagine how much worse it would have been if she and the other girls hadn't been working on their secret plan. She was glad they were in this together so that they'd be able to face the competition with confidence.

Finally, the matchmaker invited the girls into the classroom while their families waited outside. Inside, there were six tables. Each table had items laid out from previous lessons. There was an abacus, cloth and thread for embroidery, scrolls to copy, herbs for tea, admonitions to recite, and a large bowl of rice both to cook and grind into makeup.

"Girls, you have two hours to complete your tasks. No one is to exit until the two hours are finished. When the time is up, I will return with your families so we can watch you present your skills." As the matchmaker turned to leave, Mulan caught a glimpse of a familiar face behind her. Her father was walking into the courtyard! She wanted to rush out the door and hug him, but the door shut behind the matchmaker, and it was time to begin.

Mulan felt her stomach drop. What would her father think of the stunt she and the other girls were going to pull? Would he be ashamed? After traveling all the way home, would this be the welcome he deserved?

But then Mulan looked around at the eager faces of her five friends. They were a team. And she felt calmer, certain that what they were doing was best. It may not have been what those on the other side of the door would expect . . . but it was right.

When the two hours ended, the door opened and the matchmaker entered, followed by the girls' families. The matchmaker's eyes bulged. No amount of makeup could cover the shock on her face.

Mulan, Ying, Chen, Na, Mei, and Jin had pushed the individual tables together in the center of the room. Instead of six groups of tasks to judge, there was only one. The girls had taken turns grinding the rice for one bowl of makeup, which now powdered their faces flawlessly. One scroll was laid on the table, its calligraphy copied masterfully with strokes from six different hands. One large dish of perfectly cooked rice sat on the table as well. One pot of tea, made from herbs the girls had selected together, steeped next to the rice. Six pieces of fabric were stitched together to form one cloth, which was embroidered in a detailed flower pattern.

On another scroll of parchment, next to the abacus, was a series of calculations. Mulan knew all the answers were correct, because each girl had taken a turn solving while another checked her work.

The matchmaker took in the scene. She grabbed the selections of admonitions the girls were supposed to memorize. "Well, it seems the students have gone for a different approach to my teachings." Mulan could see that the matchmaker was struggling to keep her cool. "They are trying very hard to act clever, which is indeed a skill, but not one that will get them a match." She smirked at the girls. "We'll determine a winner based on the admonitions."

The matchmaker began with Mei, asking her to recite the first admonition. Mei did not speak alone. Instead, the girls all answered in unison.

The matchmaker's face reddened in anger. She moved past Mei to Jin, asking for the second admonition. Once again, the girls recited the admonition together. It was all they could manage to not break out into Mei's silly song.

Mulan could almost see steam boiling from the matchmaker's ears. The woman crumpled up the paper with the admonitions and tossed it into the bowl of rice powder makeup. The matchmaker turned to the families in the audience. "They're *your* daughters," she shouted. "Good luck!" And with that, the matchmaker marched out.

Mulan, Jin, Na, Mei, Chen, and Ying embraced. Pulling out of the hug, Mulan snuck a glance at her family. Her grandmother was smiling a knowing smile. Her mother's eyebrows were raised in an amused expression. But her father . . . her father was beaming at her.

"What a lovely welcome home!" he said cheerfully. The girls giggled nervously.

Mei's mother stepped forward. "I didn't want to say anything that might ruin the girls' lessons, but I've actually heard that this matchmaker has lost favor with a lot of families in recent years. These classes were a way for her to try and rebuild her reputation. I felt sorry for the woman and figured the training wouldn't hurt. I think our daughters have made it clear, though, that they'd be better served by a different matchmaker when the time arrives."

The six girls cried out together, "Yes!" Mulan's father gave a loud laugh in response. Then, slowly, the rest of the parents and grandparents joined in, until everyone in the room was laughing, even Ying's parents. No one had been dishonored today.

Mulan rushed forward to greet her father, and the other girls did the same with their parents.

"Father, I can't believe you're actually

here!" Mulan's happiness exploded inside her like fireworks.

Her father squinted at her. "Who is that? Is that Mulan?"

"What do you mean? Of course it is!" she exclaimed.

Her father took the sleeve of his robe and brushed it gently across his daughter's face. White powder dropped from Mulan's skin. "That's more like it. There's my girl," he said, wrapping her in a hug. Mulan nestled into his arms, breathing in his smell that she'd missed for so many months.

The families left Mei's house and walked toward the village, each girl chatting excitedly about what they'd been learning from each other over the last several weeks.

"I'm proud of you, Mulan," her father said. "While I was fighting for China, it looks like you've been fighting a small battle of your own here at home. Where did you learn to be so bold and brave?"

Mulan blushed. "I've learned everything from you and Mother and Grandmother." Grandmother Fa put an arm around Mulan, and Mulan's mother chuckled.

"Well, then, we can't let the learning stop now, can we?" Mulan's father said. "I've got a lot of lessons to make up for, since I've been away for so long." He smiled. "Where should I begin?"

Mulan's eye caught sight of movement near the schoolhouse. There, again, was the group of boys, leaping and kicking in the air.

She pointed at them. "Begin by teaching me that," Mulan said with a wide grin.

Author's Note

When I set out to work on *Mulan's Secret Plan*, I knew I had a challenge ahead of me beyond just telling the story. I had to research what the world around young Mulan might have looked like in her time—what would she eat, what would she do for fun, how would she spend her afternoons, how would she dress . . . what would she know? What made this research particularly tricky is that the legend of Mulan, as well as Disney's film, is not set in a particular decade or even century. It pulls its influence and setting from multiple centuries and dynasties in ancient China.

Therefore, while I took care to imbue Mulan's story with a sense of historical possibility, it would not be right to say that this exact story could have taken place in a particular concrete time. My focus was to make Mulan's story interesting, meaningful, and relatable to the young people who will read it—without making it completely unlikely (historically speaking!).

In ancient China, depending on the era,

school and educational opportunities were reserved for boys and men, nobles, and the aristocracy, while young women were taught domestic skills in the home. It's unlikely that a matchmaker class like the one in this story would have taken place in real life, but if it had, I feel quite sure that Mulan wouldn't have been very happy being denied an education while the boys got to learn. And she'd certainly have done something about it!

—*Tessa Roehl*